BIGGER BITES FOR
**NIBBLES**
BIGGER READERS!

# BAD BUSTER

Being bad was what
Buster did best. Until his
dad thought of a way
to sort him out.

# BAD BUSTER

Buster Reed is in the doghouse!

**Sofie Laguna**

Illustrated by Leigh Hobbs

RUNNING PRESS
**KIDS**
PHILADELPHIA·LONDON

Printed in Canada

9  8  7  6  5  4  3  2  1
Digit on the right indicates the number of this printing

Library of Congress Control Number: 2005928805

ISBN-13: 978-0-7624-2626-3
ISBN-10: 0-7624-2626-8

Original design by Marina Messiha
and Melissa Frasier, Penguin Design Studio.
Additional design for this edition by Frances J. Soo Ping Chow

Typography: Comic Sans, DaddyOhip,
MetaPlus, and New Century School Book

This book may be ordered by mail from the publisher.
Please include $2.50 for postage and handling.
***But try your bookstore first!***

This edition published by Running Press Kids, an imprint of
Running Press Book Publishers
125 South Twenty-second Street
Philadelphia, Pennsylvania 19103-4399

Visit us on the web!
www.runningpress.com

Ages 6–9
Grades 1–3

For Sue, thank you for your
encouragement – *S.L.*

For Jenny, my sister – *L.H.*

# 1
# Buster comes
# to Town

Nobody was better at being
bad than Buster Reed.

Being bad was what
Buster did best.

When Buster first came
to town with his family,
it didn't take long for

everybody to find that out.

Buster Reed flicked paint . . .

said rude words to girls . . .

stuck chewing gum under the
seat . . . wore the same socks
every day for a month . . .

and wrote his name on the desk with a crayon.

When the teacher in class said, "Buster Reed, do you know the answer?" Buster just poked out his tongue and said "No!"

Buster was so busy being bad that he was having a bit of trouble making new friends. Nobody seemed to want to play with him.

Buster pretended he didn't mind being on his own. But he was only pretending. Buster minded very much. He wished he had a friend to play with.

# 2
# A Ride on Roger's Harley

Buster's mom, Vee, was bad too. Everyone knew she had a big skull and crossbones tattoo on her butt (Miranda Morell saw it when she was getting changed in the swimming pool changing rooms). Vee Reed

was *always* late for parent–
teacher meetings. When Vee
worked in the cafeteria she
got everybody's orders mixed

up. It made the other moms
cross. Sometimes she gave
all the kids free popsicles
when she wasn't supposed to.

Buster's dad, Roger, was even badder than that! You could *see* all his tattoos and he never even *made* it to the parent–teacher meetings.

Roger always made a lot of noise on his motorbike when he dropped Buster off at school in the morning. Sometimes he took the car spot of the principal, Mr. Meed. It made Mr. Meed cross.

11

Roger Reed spent his time

working on his Harley and

carving sculptures out of

old tree stumps. He used

a *chainsaw*!

One Friday afternoon

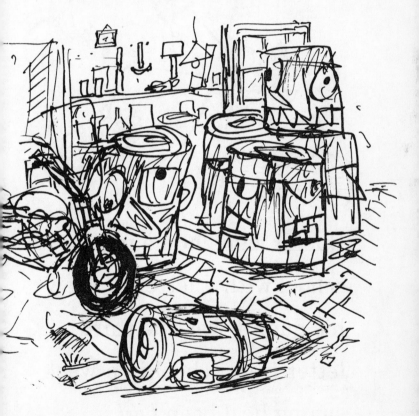

Buster came home from
school with a letter to show
his dad. It was the third
letter from school in a week
saying he'd been *bad*.

Roger stopped work on his Harley, read the note, scratched his beard and said, "Buster, I think it's time we found something to keep you out of trouble."

The next morning Roger took Buster for a ride on the Harley.

# 3
# Finding
# a Friend

Soon they came to a big
brick building with a
sign over the gate. The
sign said:

**HOME FOR LOST AND
UNWANTED DOGS**

Roger Reed rang the
bell in the office and a grey-
haired lady wearing orange
overalls and a big straw hat
came to the desk.

"Hello," she said, "how can I help you?"

"I'm Buster Reed," said Buster, "and I'm looking for something to keep me out of trouble."

"I'm Rhonda," said the lady, "and it sounds like you might be looking for a dog."

Rhonda introduced
Buster to the most lost,
most unwanted, *baddest*
bunch of dogs he had
ever seen.

Buster liked the dogs
very much.

Rhonda could see that
Buster was having a bit of
trouble deciding which one
he wanted for a friend.

"If you like," she said to
him, "you can come back

21

after school and spend
some more time with the
dogs. That might help you
to decide which one you
like the most."

And so, on his way home from school on Monday, Buster dropped into the Dogs Home . . . and the next day after that . . . and the next day after that too. Buster and the dogs got along very well.

# 4
# Buster and the Dogs

When Harry, the boxer, snarled at Buster, Buster just snarled right back. Soon Harry wagged his tail instead.

When Chester, the grumpy sausage dog,

turned his back on Buster,
Buster rubbed him under
his tummy and said, "Come
on, Chester!"

Soon Chester jumped up and ran in circles whenever he saw Buster coming.

When Shirley, the three-legged poodle, snapped at Buster, Buster just snapped right back. Soon Shirley licked Buster instead.

When Lenny, the one-eyed heeler, looked too unhappy, Buster put on his unhappiest face and tickled Lenny under the chin.

It made Lenny grin and
they both felt better.

When Linda, the postman-
chasing doberman, tried to

chase Buster, he just stood
very still and looked at her.
Soon Linda began to love
chasing the sticks Buster
threw for her instead.

Buster spent lots of time
trying to train the dogs.
He took them to the park
and tried to train them to
come when he whistled.

He never had much success but it was lots of fun practicing. Sometimes he threw the ball for them. They didn't bring it back very often.

Buster had to go and get it himself. Buster didn't mind. The dogs made him feel happy.

Buster liked Rhonda too. She didn't care about his grubby face and scabby

knees and she never
seemed to notice his smelly
socks. She was a bit smelly
herself from spending so
much time with the dogs.

Buster liked to help
Rhonda with the dogs.
Together they cleaned out
the cages . . . did lots of
washing and brushing . . .
gave the dogs food and
water . . . and took them
on big walks in the park.

Sometimes, after they'd
finished work, Rhonda took
Buster over to her cottage
next door. She showed him
all her dog books while they

ate chocolate cake and
drank tea from her best
china tea set.

Rhonda always gave
Buster as much chocolate
cake as he wanted. He
always looked very happy
when Vee and Roger came
to pick him up.

At school Buster Reed forgot to be so bad. He stopped flicking paint. He stopped saying rude words to girls. He forgot to chew gum or write his name on the desk with a crayon.

But everybody else remembered. Buster still didn't have anyone to play with.

# 5
# Buster gets a Feeling

One Thursday afternoon,
with fifteen more minutes
of school to go, Buster got
a feeling about Rhonda
and the Dogs Home. It was
a very strong sort of quivery
feeling deep in his tummy.

The feeling told him
that Rhonda and the dogs
needed him *right now*!
Buster watched the hands
of the clock and waited

for the end-of-school bell
to ring.

**At last!**

Buster ran as fast as he
could. When he got to the
Dogs Home all the dogs
were barking and howling
and scratching at their
cages. He ran through the
gate to check on the dogs.

Harry was snarling.
Chester was covering his
eyes with his paws.

Shirley was snapping. Lenny
looked angry. Linda was
running round in circles.
Something was wrong.

Where was Rhonda?
Buster heard strange
bumping noises coming
from inside her house.

He ran to the front door
and knocked very loudly.

"Rhonda!" he called.

"Rhonda!"

Nobody came. Buster
decided to have a look
through the kitchen window.
He stood on tippy toes and
peered into Rhonda's kitchen.

He couldn't see anyone.
Buster ran round the other
side of the house. He climbed
up the drain pipe and looked
through Rhonda's living-
room window.

**There were two masked
burglars in Rhonda's
living room!**

# 6
# Buster and the Burglars

Buster had to think fast.
He climbed down the drain
pipe as quickly and quietly
as he could. Next he raced
round to the dogs' kennels and
opened all the gates. He was
going to need the dogs' help.

Buster ran back to
the house with the dogs
following him. The two
burglars were climbing out

of the living-room window.
They were carrying
Rhonda's television and
her best china tea set!

"Hey you! *Stop!*" shouted
Buster.

"You can't stop us, little
kid!" the burglars shouted

back, their mouths full of Rhonda's  chocolate cake.

"No," said Buster, "but *they* can!" Buster gave his loudest whistle, and this time all the dogs came running.

The burglars tried to run away. They ran round the back of the house. The dogs chased them back. They ran down the side of the house but the dogs cut them off.

They ran down the other
side of the house and again
the dogs stopped them.

"Quick!" shouted one of
the burglars. "Up the tree!"

The burglars climbed up
the big tree in front of
Rhonda's cottage.

Buster gave another big
whistle. All the dogs stood
around the bottom of the
tree. They barked and
snapped and howled up
at the burglars.

The burglars were too
scared to move.

# 7
## "Good Dogs!"

Buster could hear the loud engine noises of two big motorbikes. It was Vee and Roger coming to pick him up.

And, look, there was Rhonda on the back of Vee's motorbike! Her arms were

full of dog food from a visit
to the pet shop.

Vee and Rhonda gave
Buster a big hug.

Roger called out to the
burglars. "Come down from
the tree!"

"We're scared of the
dogs!" they shouted back.

Buster gave one more loud whistle. The dogs came to Buster. They sat quietly.

"Good dogs!" he said.

"Now come down!" Roger called out again. "The dogs won't hurt you, they do what Buster tells them!"

Buster looked very proud.

The scared burglars climbed slowly down from the tree.

"That Buster sure is good with those dogs!" said one of the burglars to the other.

# 8
# Buster Finds Friends

The next day there was a picture of Buster and the dogs on the front page of the newspaper.

## BUSTER REED
## DOES GOOD

Suddenly Buster Reed
was the school hero. For
a little while anyway.

Now sometimes Buster

Reed is good . . .

Sometimes Buster Reed
is bad . . .

And sometimes Buster

Reed is just somewhere in between . . .

And these days Buster has lots and lots of friends . . . as well as one very special friend.

## From Sofie Laguna

Everyone in my family, except me, rides motorbikes just like Vee and Roger. I don't like riding them that much because I get scared I might fall off. I do like dogs though. I have my own dog. I found him at the Lost Dogs Home. Tigger keeps the burglars away because he barks so loudly.

Most of the time Tigger and I are pretty good. Tigger's only bad when he chases people on roller blades.

## From Leigh Hobbs

I've always liked dogs. And now I
have two. One is a kelpie called
Asta. She runs about with a ball in
her mouth all day, or a rubber foot
with a face on it.

Ruby, the other one, is a small Blue
Heeler. Ruby eats and sleeps and is
very lazy. I had both of these
animals in mind when I drew the
pictures for *Bad Buster*.

# HUNGry for More?

# HaVe a NiBBLe!